THE
SECRET SANTA
FROM THE
BLACK LAGOON®

Get more monster-sized laughs from

The Black Lagoon®

THE
SECRET SANTA
FROM THE
BLACK LAGOON®

I'D LIKE A JUICY FLY.

by Mike Thaler
Illustrated by Jared Lee

SCHOLASTIC INC.

GESUNDHEIT!

For my greatest present
my wife Patty
—M.T.

To Santa Claus
—J.L.

ISBN 978-0-545-78519-8

Text copyright © 2014 by Mike Thaler
Illustrations copyright © 2014 by Jared D. Lee Studio, Inc.

12 11 10 9 8 7 6 5 4 3 2 1   14 15 16 17 18 19/0

Printed in the U.S.A.   40
First printing, November 2014

CONTENTS

CHAPTER 1
THE PLAN

← ELF

It was the Christmas season ... again. My teacher, Mrs. Green, was very excited.

"We're going to do a 'Secret Santa' in class again this year. Everyone put your name on a little piece of paper, and drop it in the hat. Then you'll get a gift for the person you pick out."

She held up a Santa hat and jiggled it. I moaned.

"What's the matter?" asked Eric, filling out his little piece of paper.

← ERIC

7

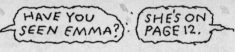

"Last year I got Penny. It was horrible. With my luck, this year I'll get another girl," I said.

"What's so bad about that?" asked Eric, while folding his piece of paper.

8

"Have you ever shopped for *a girl*?" I sighed.

"Can't say that I have," smiled Eric, taking his paper up to Mrs. Green.

I followed him. With shaking hands, I dropped my paper into the hat.

"Tomorrow, we'll pick the Secret Santas," said Mrs. Green.

CHAPTER 2
SANTA PRACTICE

After school, I was still depressed.

"Cheer up," said Eric, "the best is yet to come."

"I'm not ready for Christmas," I said.

↑ DEPRESSED ↑ MORE DEPRESSED

11

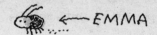

"Well, I'll help you get ready," smiled Eric.

"How?" I asked.

"We'll have a Santa practice."

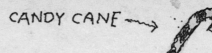
CANDY CANE ⟶

"A what?" I asked.

"A Santa practice," announced Eric. "First off, can you name four of Santa's reindeer?"

13

← BEETLE

I scratched my chin. "Paul, John, Ringo, and George," I said.

"Those aren't reindeer," said Eric. "Those are *Beatles.*"

"Oh," I said.

BORING.

14

"Next, can you do a Santa laugh?" asked Eric.

"A what?" I asked.

"Go ahead, laugh like Santa," said Eric.

"HA-HA-HA."

"Not even close," said Eric.

"HE-HE-HE," I giggled.

NOTE: THE BEATLES WERE A ROCK
BAND IN THE 1960'S.

"Worse," said Eric, taking a deep breath. "Santa laughs 'HO-HO-HO.'"

HANDS OVER STOMACH

"HOW-HOW-HOW?" I asked.

"Better," said Eric. "Now we'll have a Christmas knock-knock joke. Knock, knock," he said.

"Knock, knock," I repeated.

"No, no, you're supposed to say, 'Who's there?'"

"Who's there?" I asked.

"Nicholas," smiled Eric.

"Nicholas who?" I asked.

← SANTA SNAIL

"A nicholas not enough money
to spend on a present," laughed
Eric.

"HO-HO-HO!" I said.

HAVE YOU SEEN MAYA?

CHAPTER 3
THE LUCK OF THE DRAW

The next day in class, Mrs. Green made an announcement. "All right, class, it's time to pick our Secret Santas. We'll go alphabetically. You're first, Hubie."

Sometimes I wish my last name was *Zool*, instead of *Cool*.

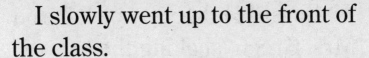
I slowly went up to the front of the class.

Mrs. Green held out the Santa cap. I closed my eyes and reached in. I could feel all the little pieces of paper with my fingers. *Which one feels like a boy's name?* I thought to myself.

OH, GREAT.

"Go on, Hubie . . . pick," said Mrs. Green, shaking the hat.

GLOVE
OF
DOOM

CHAPTER 4
THE HAND OF DOOM

I grabbed a slip and pulled it out. Then I went straight back to my seat. I slowly opened the paper and stared at it. My face turned green.

WHO DID YOU GET?

IS IT A GIRL?

OH, NO!

DON'T MIND ME.

TAKE A DEEP BREATH, HUBIE.

21

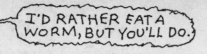

I had picked—Mrs. Green!
My eyes glazed over.

"Who did you pick?" asked
Eric.

"He can't tell," declared Penny,
"it's a *Secret* Santa."

IN
SHOCK →

HIS FACE
IS STILL
GREEN.

CHAPTER 5
BUSTED

On the bus ride home, everybody held their little piece of paper tightly in their fists. Nobody was talking, except Eric.

I'M GOING TO EAT THAT NUMBER IN THE CORNER.

23

"So who'd ya pick?" he asked.

"I'll show you mine, if you show me yours."

"He can't tell," piped up Penny, "it's against the rules!"

I just sat there looking straight ahead. I couldn't blink all the way home. I was in shock!

CHAPTER 6

BUMMED AND NUMBED

When I got home, I went right to my room and fell on my bed. Mom came in and sat down.

"What's wrong, Hubie?" she asked.

DISTRAUGHT

I buried my head in the pillow. "Come on, Hubie, it can't be that bad!"

"It is—it is! Out of all the people in my class, I picked Mrs. Green for Secret Santa!"

"So?"

"I have to buy her a gift!"

"So?"

"I have no idea what she would like, and if I did, I probably couldn't afford it."

"I'll help you, Hubie," she said, patting my head. "We'll go shopping together."

NOT SUPPOSED
TO BE IN THIS
BOOK

27

CHAPTER 7

NO BALL AT THE MAUL

The mall was already decorated for Christmas. There were lots of reindeer, and elves, tinsel, and trees, and tons of Santas. There were tall Santas, small Santas, fat Santas, thin Santas, jolly Santas, and grim Santas. There was one at every store and two at every door.

Christmas comes earlier every year. Eventually it will start right after New Year's!

AN ELF IS SMALLER THAN A SECOND GRADER.

While "Jingle Bells" played, we went from store to store. The mall had everything from suits to boots. From hats to bats. It was a world of things. Blue things. Red things. Foot things, head things. Things that click, things that buzz, things with fur, things with fuzz. I saw lots of things that I would like for myself!

Radio-controlled race cars, a computer super game center, a wrist radio. Buying a gift for myself would be easy. Buying one for Mrs. Green was impossible.

"Mom, at Christmas, why doesn't everyone just buy their own presents? That way everyone would get what they wanted."

"Because that is not what Christmas is about, Hubie. Christmas is about *giving*, not *receiving*."

"Well, you could still give. It would just be to yourself."

"Hubie, Christmas is about making others happy—not yourself."

I LOVE IT!

TO ME

FROM ME

HUBIE IMAGINING

"It's succeeded," I grumbled. "I'm miserable."

BUMMER.

CHAPTER 8
AROUND THE WORLD

ISN'T THIS FUN, HUBIE.

I'M RUNNING OUT OF STEAM, MOM.

LET'S GO HOME.

On we searched from one shop to another, till the mall was closing. There were lots of things, but they were either too big, too small, too bright, too dull, too cheap, or too expensive. Every time I found something I thought Mrs. Green would like, Mom said, "Not appropriate."

LOBSTER BUG ←

Nothing in Sports World was appropriate. Nothing in Vicky's Secret World was appropriate, or Pet World, or Shoe World, or Coat World, or Kitchen World, or Appliance World.

"We've searched all the Worlds, Mom, and nothing's appropriate. Let's go home."

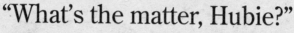

CHAPTER 9
GRAND BY HAND

"What's the matter, Hubie?"

"I'm depressed," I said.

"Don't be, Hubie. Why don't you make Mrs. Green something?"

"I can't make shoes. I can't make a dress. I can't make a computer."

"You could make a painting. You are a good artist," said Mom, putting her arm around me.

"Hmmm," I said, "I am a good artist."

36

"And something someone's made means a lot more than something someone's bought," Mom said.

"Not to me, Mom, but I'm desperate."

CHAPTER 10
GENIUS AT WORK

I went right to my room and got a clean piece of paper and all the markers I could find. Then I looked down at the blank piece of paper.

38

What would Mrs. Green like best?

A painting of a fighter plane, a rocket ship, a robot, an explosion?

Wait, I'll do my best painting—a rainbow-colored dinosaur.

I carefully started drawing the outline of a T-Rocks. When the outline was done, I painted the head yellow, the neck orange, the back red, the side blue, the bottom purple, and the legs green.

Then I stepped back and held up my thumb.

"It's beautiful."

Then I took it to show Mom.

"It's beautiful!" she smiled.

MAGNIFICENT.

PAINT

HUBIE VAN GOGH

41

CHAPTER 11
FRAMED

The next day I was about to roll up my drawing and tie a ribbon around it.

"Wait!" called Mom. She pulled a frame from behind her back.

"Ta da!" she exclaimed. "A beautiful painting like that should have a frame."

"Like in a museum?" I asked.

"Like in a museum," smiled Mom.

43

CHAPTER 12
STRAIGHT FROM THE REINDEER'S MOUTH

"Tell me about Christmas, Mom."

"Well, Hubie, Christmas as we know it today started out with the feast day of Saint Nicholas in Europe. Saint Nicholas was a kindly saint who lived in Turkey— not the North Pole."

A LITTLE TOWN IN TURKEY

45

HAVE YOU SEEN ROY? I'M TRYING TO REACH HIM ON HIS CELL PHONE?

"Is that why we have turkey on Christmas?" I asked.

"I'm not sure," said Mom.

"I'm glad he didn't live in Greece," I said.

EXCUSE ME, CAN YOU BEND DOWN?

AX

"Well, anyway," continued Mom. "On his feast day in December people put nuts, apples, and candy in shoes left around the house."

"Sneaker treats? That sounds unsanitary to me," I grumbled.

"Dutch and German colonists continued this practice in the New World."

"How did it turn into our Christmas?" I asked.

48

PIMPLE PILOT

"I bet malls helped a lot, too."

"They probably did, Hubie, but it's a great idea. A season where people are kind to one another, and think more about others than about themselves."

MOM, THIS IS GETTING TOO MUSHY.

"Mom, I wish Christmas would last all year round," I said.

"So do I," sighed Mom.

50

I'M SO HAPPY TO SEE YOU.

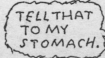

TELL THAT TO MY STOMACH.

CHAPTER 13
HUBIE CLAUS

That night I had a dream. I was in the North Pole and I was Santa Claus. Instead of making toys, all the elves and I were drawing rainbow dinosaurs. Then I got in my sleigh, which was a red race car. All the reindeer got in with me and we drove through Christmas night delivering rainbow dinosaur pictures to every kid in the world. On Christmas morning, when they all opened their presents a loud "phooey!" sounded throughout the world. Nobody liked their present. Hate mail flooded in.

I don't believe in you anymore said the letters.

CHAPTER 14
PRESENTS OF MIND

The day of our party finally arrived. Everyone brought in their presents and set them on their desks. One by one, they handed them to the person they had picked. I was first so I walked up to Mrs. Green's desk and handed her my drawing, wrapped in rainbow paper. She slowly opened it and went, "Ohhhhh."

BULLY
BUG →

Then she held it up for all the class to see. They all went, "Ohhhhh."

"It's beautiful, Hubie," smiled Mrs. Green, wiping a tear from the corner of her eye. "It's just what I always wanted. I will put it up on the wall behind my desk and keep it forever. Someday it might be worth a million dollars when you are a famous artist."

I went back to my desk and sat smiling as all the other kids opened their presents. Freddy got a spoon, Doris got a music box with a little ballerina on top that twirled to the music. Penny got a compass, Eric got a joke book, Derek got a baseball cap, and Randy got a slide rule.

59

I felt so good already. I was surprised when Mrs. Green came up to me. She was holding a big box.

"This is your present, Hubie," she smiled.

The whole class stood around me as I unwrapped the big box. I opened the top, reached in, and pulled out a bright red radio-controlled race car.

"Ohhh," said everyone.
"Ohhh," I said, "it's just what I wanted."

And it was.